# CHARLIE, THE LOST DOG

D0055122

**Other Apple Paperbacks
you will enjoy:**

*A Dog Called Lucky Tide*
by William Koehler

*Hi, Fella*
by Era Zistel

*Kavik the Wolf Dog*
by Walt Morey

*The Mystery at Wolf River*
by Mary Frances Shura

*Nobody's Dog*
by Lynn Hall

*Orphaned Pup*
by Eleanor J. Lapp

*Swimmer*
by Harriet May Savitz

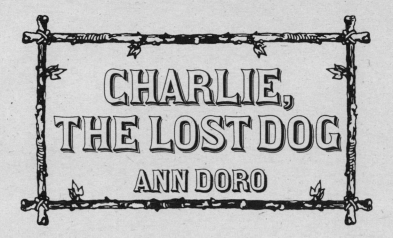

# CHARLIE, THE LOST DOG

## ANN DORO

AN
**APPLE**
PAPERBACK

SCHOLASTIC INC.
New York Toronto London Auckland Sydney

ISBN 0-590-42479-3

12 11 10 9 8 7 6 5 4 3 2 1          0 1 2 3 4 5/9

Printed in the U.S.A.          40

First Scholastic printing, March 1990

*To my children,*
*Marie and Ed Gravage*

# 1

As far as Charlie was concerned, they'd been in the car too long. He whined and nuzzled Maggie's neck. She turned in her seat and put her hands on either side of his head, holding it to her face.

"He knows something's wrong, Mom."

"Not wrong, darling. Just different."

The dog whined again, and tried to climb into the front of the car. Claire Dawson held out her arm to restrain him.

"No, Charlie!" she said.

"He knows he's going to be left behind."

"Maggie," her mother said firmly, "we've gone over this before. If we did take him with us, he'd be held in quarantine for six months. He'd hate that. He'll be perfectly happy with Uncle Ray and your cousins."

"Aunt Fern will always be asking him if he wiped his feet before he came into the house. And

Uncle Ray'll have a fit if he chases the sheep."

"Maggie! I *have* to do this job."

Maggie frowned. Her green eyes looked almost gray. She tossed her curly red ponytail as she ruffled the thick black and buff fur of Charlie's shoulder.

"I don't see why your dumb company had to send *you* to Hawaii. Can't somebody over there do those pineapple commercials?"

Claire Dawson smiled, letting her hand rest for a moment on her daughter's.

"Most girls your age would love the idea of playing on the beach in the islands. It'll be warm and sunny, perfect for swimming. Of course, you'll be in school while I'm working. . . ."

"But Mom! I won't know *anybody!* And I'll only get more freckles being on the beach." Her head turned momentarily as she saw a horse in a nearby field. "Why does it have to take so long?"

"It's my job to interview children for the hula numbers, and I have to choose locations and . . . you know all that goes into it. We're doing a whole sequence so I won't have to go back for a while."

"Charlie's going to forget all about me."

"No, he won't. He'll have the time of his life on the ranch, but a good German shepherd is always loyal to his own people. And Charlie's the best of his breed."

She rolled the window down to let the dog put his head out. "You like the feel of the wind in your face, don't you boy? Hmm — cool for the first of October."

They drove in silence for a time, watching the changes in scenery as they gained altitude. Spreading branches of live oak trees shaded a few cattle, their leaves remaining green while the occasional black oak displayed a show of yellow leaves about to fall. Further on, the oaks thinned and a thick stand of pine forest stretched away on either side.

"We're higher, Mom," Maggie commented, noting a sign that read Pioneer, elevation 2,951. They drove through the small mountain community.

"I think we're passing through the gold rush country," her mother commented.

Road signs confirmed this: Gold Mine Road, the mileage to Angel's Camp, Roaring Camp Recreation Area, and gold panning equipment advertised for sale.

The road dipped into a grassy meadow. On the left a barn-red house with a sharply peaked roof was screened by a carefully trimmed hedge. Signs of civilization, however, were few. The outstanding one was the well-surfaced asphalt road over which they drove.

"Look at that old shack," Maggie pointed out. "It looks like it's falling down."

"I'd like to take that weathered wood home with us to line the den," Mrs. Dawson said.

A logging truck came down the mountain road toward them. Three huge logs were chained to its flat bed. A wall rose behind it, as if the highway had been cut out of solid granite.

"Look, Mom! Trees growing right out of the rock," Maggie exclaimed.

There were yellow-and-black deer-crossing signs, and one, similar but with the familiar pedestrian pictured, warned that people might be crossing in the next two miles. They came down the grade to Silver Lake, its water shimmering blue. Gray clouds were beginning to form above it.

Charlie became restless, moving back and forth in the rear seat. Maggie reached for his ears and kissed the side of his nose.

"I'm with you, Charlie!" she said. "This trip's the pits."

He turned around several times, then settled down and closed his eyes.

A road maintenance crew was clearing a rock slide. The flagman signaled them to a halt, allowing several cars from the opposite direction to pass.

"I hope this won't hold us up too long," Mrs. Dawson said anxiously, looking up at the sky. Maggie had just commented on a sign that read

Autos and Pickups, Snow Tires OK, Carry Chains.

"It couldn't mean now," she said. "It never snows before November, does it Mom?"

"I hope not," her mother answered, proceeding cautiously past the work area as the flagman waved them on. "Try to get a weather report, will you?"

Maggie fiddled with the dial, got a rock station, an afternoon talk show, and a burst of static.

"Not much here," she said, turning back to the music and bouncing to its beat.

A road led off to the right, with signs pointing toward Kit Carson Lodge.

"We could get gas there," Maggie said. "And I'm hungry." But she said it as the car was passing the turn.

"We'll watch for the next place," her mother said, down shifting for another steep climb.

They passed an historical marker that told of a maiden's grave in the vicinity.

"Wonder if her folks were in the gold rush," Maggie said. "It must have been really bad traveling in those days."

"We're at seven thousand feet now," her mother said. "It can't be too much farther to Monitor's Pass." She leaned forward to study the increasing clouds. "They say it's closed in winter." She sighed. "I don't like the look of the sky."

"Gas station over there," Maggie said. "Bet we can get sandwiches, too."

Mrs. Dawson drummed her fingernails on the steering wheel, glancing at the cluster of cars ahead of her at the pumps. Another car pulled in just behind them. When they had gotten the tank filled, she pulled across the lot to where sections of huge logs marked parking for the Kirkwood Inn. Blue, red, yellow, and gray-green banners flapped in the brisk wind.

Charlie leaped out after Maggie, ready to play. Together they investigated cords of wood stacked near a rock wall leading up to a brick chimney.

"Here, Charlie!" Mrs. Dawson commanded. Nose to ground, he paid no attention. "Charlie!" She took his collar and led him to a spot near the car. "Now stay!"

She and Maggie went inside, Mrs. Dawson turning at the door to make sure Charlie was still sitting in his spot.

"Good dog," she approved.

While they waited for hamburgers, Maggie went to the smoke-blackened fireplace, reaching her hands toward the leaping flames. Then she turned and studied two men seated at a nearby table. They were dressed in heavy jackets, had long hair and beards. She looked at her mother,

6

slim in her jeans and sweater, her dark hair cut short and fitting smoothly around her face.

"I like how you look, Mom," she said in a sudden burst of pride as she crossed to pick up her sandwich from the counter.

"Why, thank you," her mom said, smiling. Then she spoke to the young man behind the counter.

"It's clouding up outside. Surely it's not going to snow, is it?"

Busy, he tossed an answer over his shoulder. "Don't count on it. We were snowed in the end of September a few years back."

Mrs. Dawson made no comment, but her face settled into a frown. While her mother paid the bill, Maggie took her 'burger out to share it with Charlie. He was nowhere in sight.

"Charlie! Goodies," she called.

She spied him behind the huge woodpile. He sniffed and scratched the dirt, as if trying to get at something under the wood. When he smelled meat in her outstretched hand, he bounded over, almost knocking her mother down as she came out of the inn. He gulped the offering and wagged his tail, begging for more.

"Let's get going," Mrs. Dawson said as she slid behind the wheel. "If it does happen to snow, I want to be over the summit before it begins."

She reached back to open a door for the dog. "In, Charlie," she said.

Instead, he headed back to the woodpile. Maggie ran after him.

"For heaven's sake, Maggie! He's had obedience school."

Maggie said nothing, but took Charlie's collar and led him back to the car.

Her mother seemed preoccupied as she pulled out onto the highway. She fiddled with the radio dial. The only thing that came in now was an interview program.

"Not even any music!" Maggie complained. "Just static." She reached to turn it off, but Mrs. Dawson stopped her.

"Maybe they'll have some news."

The wind had become stronger and colder. Mrs. Dawson rolled the window up, and Charlie became restless again.

"He's tired of being in this old car," Maggie said. "So'm I."

"I know he's cramped back there. When we got him last Christmas, he could curl up on your lap and go to sleep."

Charlie made himself as comfortable as possible and dozed. An occasional small *woof* indicated he might be dreaming.

They drove on, the miles of mountain forest seeming endless. A helicopter hovered over a burned area where black skeleton trees stood against a sand-colored mountain.

"What's the 'copter doing there? The fire's out."

"Sometimes a fire will smolder and burst out again. Maybe there'll be something on the news . . . if we can get it," Mrs. Dawson said as she turned off on Highway 89, heading toward Markleeville. A few snowflakes drifted down.

"Snow, Mom!" Maggie exclaimed. "Maybe we can let Charlie out to play in it."

"I don't think there'll be enough for you to romp in," her mother said. But she looked worried, and although the speed limit was posted at 55 miles per hour, she speeded up to 65. A herd of cattle huddled under tall pine trees on the right. High barbed-wire fences bordered the highway on both sides.

"We're climbing again. Maggie, look at the map. See if you can tell how far to Monitor's Pass."

She turned on the windshield wipers to clear away the gently falling flakes of snow. An urgent voice broke in on the program, interrupted by bursts of static. "High winds . . . heavy snow . . . chains . . . summit areas unsafe . . . motorists advised . . ."

"Oh, no!"

Maggie followed her mother's gaze to a red light on the instrument panel. The word *oil* stood out against the light. Her mother looked scared. Maggie felt a tightness in her stomach, wondering what they would do. She knew you couldn't drive a car without oil. Her cousin had let his car run out once, and they said his engine froze.

"Are we, I mean — that red light — is it bad?"

Her mother said nothing. She pulled over into a place where a forest service road led back among the trees. It was blocked by a big green metal gate. Turning off the ignition, she opened the door and ran back to look in the trunk. She left the door standing open, and Charlie, roused by the sound of tires crunching on gravel, sprang over the seat and out.

"Keep him with you," Claire Dawson called as she rummaged through the trunk. "Why didn't I think to have them check the oil back there?"

Charlie sniffed. The falling snowflakes seemed to tickle his nose. Maggie brushed snow from the saddle of thick black hair that stretched over his back and down over the buff fur of his sides.

"Maggie, turn up the radio so I can hear it, please. Try to get that station more clearly." Mrs. Dawson lifted a rolled blanket and pulled out a can of oil.

"Thank goodness!"

She hurried to the front of the car, then asked, "Can you pull that lever under the dash on the driver's side?"

Maggie yanked the lever, then turned up the volume. The newscaster's voice boomed a single word before his message became garbled in static. "Blizzard!"

"We've got to get out of here!"

Maggie looked at her mother, then at the snow. It was falling faster, and the wind was whipping it around. This was no adventure.

"Charlie," she called. "Come! Get in the car."

But Charlie had spied a rabbit on the other side of the gate. He ran and jumped. Maggie watched in dismay as he cleared it and disappeared among the trees.

"Charlie! Charlie!" Maggie cried, over and over again.

"Here, Charlie. Come!" her mother shouted in her most authoritative voice.

The dog did not appear.

# 2

Charlie heard their frantic cries, but paid no attention. He had been cooped up in the car too long. It felt wonderful to stretch his legs. And he was intent upon trailing the rabbit. He would run, stop to sniff, then dash on.

"Charlie!" he heard from a distance. But the pure joy of racing in the chill air spoke to him louder than the cries of his people. The boredom of the ride fell away as he ran on through the trees. He had no idea of time, but could feel in his breathing that he'd gone a long way. He paused, panting. Then he plunged down a ravine, splashing into a stream before he could halt his downward rush.

A shout came from far away. Part of him wanted to answer it and go back, to obey the command he could hardly hear. But an urge inside was forcing him on. He sniffed about to find the scent of that small animal with big ears. He loved the feel of the wind all around him, not just from the car window. He continued to run among dry ferns, weeds, seedling manzanita, under tall pine trees, and aspen with golden leaves. Snow fell from the sky and dropped from every bush he touched. It was rapidly covering the thick pad of dead leaves on the ground. He could not know the time he was squandering was so important.

The temperature was dropping. The wetness from the brook reached high up his long legs, causing him to run as much to warm himself as to chase the wild thing. The wind was becoming a frightening force, throwing the fast falling snow into his eyes, pushing the coldness deep into his body.

Whining, he lowered his head, sniffing to find his own scent and follow it back to the warm car and the people who cared for him. With a momentary lull in the wind, he heard them faintly calling. He barked in response, but the wind whipped up again, hurling his sound back to him.

# 3

**M**om, we can't leave him! He'll die."

Maggie shivered. She grasped the bars of the gate in her fingers, as if to yank it open and run to find him. But it was padlocked.

"Charlie! Charlie!" she called out, "Come back! Come back!"

Her voice was hoarse from shouting. Her mother called out, too. Mrs. Dawson looked at the ground, with the snow well up over their jogging shoes. She looked at her watch. The snow was falling so heavily they could barely see the trees.

"Maggie, it's been over half a hour. And the storm is getting worse."

With the howling wind, snow was being driven into their faces. Mrs. Dawson pulled the hood of Maggie's jacket up over her head and pulled a scarf from her neck to cover her own. She looked at her watch again. The radio blared fitfully. No complete message came through.

"We can't wait any longer. If the road gets

14

blocked, it will be days before anyone gets up this way. It's probably going to be closed, like it said on the map."

"Mom, no!" Maggie screamed, clinging to the gate. "He'll come back. He always has."

"It's snowing too hard," her mother said. Then, quietly, "We can't give him any more time. If we're stranded here, we'll freeze."

There was sadness in her eyes and a determination Maggie had never seen before. She allowed her hands to be pulled gently away from the cold metal. Numbly, she followed her mother to the car.

"We should be able to get to Markleeville. The sheriff there may be able to find him after the storm, Maggie."

Tears welled in Maggie's eyes. "I'll never see him again. I know I won't," she sobbed.

# 4

Charlie raced about blindly, sniffing the white cover and finding no scent at all. He had never experienced anything like this, never had to rely on instinct before. He circled about, his paws sinking deep into the snow. Something told him to keep moving, to try to find the car and the loving hands of the girl who cared for him. He climbed up a slope. Snow dropped from the bushes he blundered into, often covering his face. He shook and kept going on. Time seemed endless to him. At last he found the gate and cleared it with a powerful leap. He tried to see the car through the blizzard, and to find his people, who would give him good food and a drink of water. He wanted to curl up at the foot of the girl's bed and go to sleep.

For the first time in his year of life, Charlie felt lonely. There had been a vague remembrance of missing his mother. But his people made friendly sounds to him. They petted him and roughhoused with him. There had been warm bowls of milk. Everything there had been warm. Everything here was cold, and getting colder and whiter all the time.

Pacing back and forth, he cried his sadness. Finally, in desperation, he threw back his head and howled. There was no answering call. He was alone in a place that was at once frightening and exciting. A place with trees everywhere and smells that sharpened the instinct to track and hunt which, at home, had only been teased by squirrels chattering in the one big tree.

He couldn't find any smells now. The snow had fallen so fast it was halfway up to his belly. Without knowing it, he stood in the spot where Maggie had stood and called him over an hour before. He waited by the gate for some time, whining and howling now and then. At last, feeling the emptiness that told him it was dinnertime, he leaped back over the gate and ran into the forest.

He couldn't run fast. The snow was so deep he had to lunge through it. He had never hunted, but his growing appetite urged him to watch for animals. When he did catch sight of a mouse in a bare spot under a tree, he was too slow. The animal disappeared into some invisible hole. Another animal appeared briefly, prompting him to bark with eagerness. It ran, and the snow covered its tracks. Pushing forward, sniffing and yipping from time to time, he came at last to a small building.

He rushed to it and pawed at the door. When there was no response, he began to bark loudly as he caught the people smell. The door opened abruptly, and a man peered out. His gray hair hung to his shoulders, and a thick, matted beard hung over the front of his heavy shirt. His eyes squinted, and he scowled.

"What you want? Git, now! Git away from here."

In answer, Charlie whined and pushed forward.

"Git! We don't have nothing for you. Betsy and me got just enough for ourselves."

Charlie felt warmth coming out the door and tried to force his way in. The smell became stronger. It reminded him of the man who brought letters to the woman at home. The man who hurried into the yard every morning, and always backed out the gate when he left. The same scent of fear was coming from this old man. He held a big stick in his rough hand. *Whack!* He brought it down on the dog's nose.

"Now git!"

The painful blow made Charlie's nose throb, and with the hurt came a twinge of loneliness for his own people. They would never hit him. They would not shut the door on him. But they were gone.

His feet were heavy as he slunk away, his tail between his legs, his head lowered. He went around the corner of the cabin, hoping to find a spot out of the wind where he could rest.

At the back of the cabin there was a shelter of sorts, some wide boards leaning against the cabin. The space was closed at one end. Grateful to be out of the snow, Charlie slipped inside. As his eyes grew accustomed to the darkness, they took in a bin nailed to the cabin wall and a bucket standing near it. Straw rustled under his feet.

Looking around, he discovered the source of a new smell. Another animal lived in the lean-to. It was much taller than he, and it stood motionless on four legs. His instinct had already told him that living creatures were to be his meat. But not this one. Too big!

The size of the animal threatened him, but the snow had made his feet sore. It hurt to walk. He was not going any further. Making sure of a way to escape, he moved as near the warmth of the unknown animal as he dared. Too worn out to heed the growling of his stomach, he dropped onto the straw bedding. He slept and dreamed of a girl with gentle hands.

# 5

Caleb slumped on the three-legged stool. Leaning his elbows on the rough pine table, he held his head in his hands.

"Been some while since you felt called upon to hit a dog."

Without the company of another human being, sometimes for months on end, the old man spent a great deal of time talking to himself. He stared at the yellowing photograph of his mother, which he kept across from his place at the table. How many years had it been since he'd seen her? How many years had he spent wandering and searching before giving up his dream and settling in this remote cabin? His father had spoken of a family gold claim, and the gold *his* grandfather had taken from it during the California gold rush. Caleb had been so certain, when he ran away from home at age fifteen, he could find a fortune in the mother lode. Forced, years later, to admit failure, he was too proud to go back.

"I didn't want the gold mainly for myself. It was supposed to be for her."

He stared at the picture, wishing it could talk. He had left the small town in Illinois back in 1930, determined to find a way to ease the poverty in which the family had been forced to live. After the Great Depression had broken his father's spirit, it seemed the only one who could provide was Caleb. At least that was how he saw it at the time. Besides his parents, he had left behind two younger sisters and a baby brother. He had no idea where they might be now, or whether they still lived.

The gold! How it dazzled. Stories of his great grandfather had stirred him, and he would look for hours at the nugget the family treasured. At last it had gone to buy flour and beans. That was when he had gone off to search for gold.

"Look at yourself! Your sixty-ninth birthday, and all you've got to recommend yourself is a mangy old mule, a shack, and the skins from the animals you trap so you can eat."

He had always hunted to supply their needs, but his hands, twisted with arthritis, found it hard to hold a gun steady anymore. He didn't like to trap animals, and did it only because the meat fed him, and the sale of furs bought grain for Betsy. He would not stint on the mule's needs. She had followed him faithfully, carrying supplies on the old wooden pack saddle during their years of wandering. She deserved whatever he could give her.

"Quit bemoaning your fate, you flea-bitten old coot. You can give the dog a bite of meat and a bone to chew. And, like everybody else, he'll be on his way. But at least you can forget about hitting him."

Caleb's grumpiness covered the ache of loneliness in his heart and the ache of arthritis in his hands. He stomped over to the ancient wood-burning stove and poured the last of the coffee into his cup. Holding it high, he sang, "Happy birthday to me."

# 6

Charlie wakened slowly. He became aware of a loud braying noise. Something nudged him. As he lifted his head, his nose bumped into a much larger nose. The big long-eared thing brayed again, and showed its huge teeth. Snarling, the dog sprang to his feet and backed away.

"Hold your hosses, Betsy."

Charlie heard the call coming from the cabin. The animal threw its head up and down, pawing the straw with one hoof. Dust flew everywhere. It tickled the dog's nose. Charlie sneezed. The strange creature blew air out between its lips in a burbling snort, and pawed some more. It skittered back and forth, not coming any closer.

"You cantankerous old mule, quit your belly-aching."

The voice brought back the memory of the painful stick. Charlie whined. His nose throbbed anew from the encounter with the mule's inquiring face. He didn't want any more of the stick or the mule.

Its behavior made him uneasy. He turned and made a dash for the entrance.

*Smack!* His nose hurt all over again as he ran into the old man. Caleb fell, sinking into the snow. Charlie dodged away, struggling over a drift piled almost as high as the lean-to.

"Consarn you anyway! Git away from here!" Caleb bellowed, shaking an angry fist after the dog.

Charlie didn't need to be told. His feet dug deep holes in the snow as he scrambled away. He heard the old man muttering to himself.

"Cussed critter! . . . Leastways, he don't seem to want to bite."

The dog took a quick look back, decided he wasn't being followed, skidded down the other side of the drift and let himself stop to look around.

A glittering expanse of whiteness stretched before him. There was an open space in front of the cabin. Here and there a stump poked up out of the show. Beyond the clearing were trees, trees, trees! The sun sparkled on snow layering the branches of fir, pine, and cedar. Other trees, bare of leaves, held snow along their branches. Excitement stirred in the dog. There was much about this forest he did not understand, but he was eager to learn.

His nose, the part that helped him most, caught an enticing whiff of something under a nearby sugar pine. He found a nice-sized knucklebone. The scent told him the meat had been cooked. The smell of the old man was there, too.

When Caleb came around the corner of the log cabin a few minutes later, Charlie watched with wary eyes. But he did not stop gnawing on the bone. He was ready to fight, if necessary, to keep it. But the man paid no attention. He picked up a shovel standing on the single step of the cabin, harrumphed, and went back toward the shed, scolding at Betsy.

In a little while, he came back to the step. He picked up some snowshoes and strapped them to his feet. They reminded Charlie of Maggie's tennis racquet. He wanted to tell his loneliness in a whine. But he feared the man's stick.

He chewed every scrap of meat from the bone. Then he dug a hole in the snow and buried it for later. The world was calling, and he couldn't wait.

As he packed the snow down around his bone, he saw that the man had picked up a gun. Charlie didn't know what it was, but he wanted no more encounters with sticks, or anything that looked like one. He didn't wait for Caleb to decide to use it. He ran off into the forest.

The snow had hardened on top of the drifts. Part of the time he ran easily over the crust. Then his paws would break through, and a leg would sink deep into the snow. Each time, he floundered.

He would pull the leg out and scratch to get footing.

Drifts had been piled high by the furious wind of the night before, and there were bare spots where the snow had been blown away. Charlie noticed the tracks of other animals in the snow. They were easy to follow. His nose discovered so many scents he ran this way and that, squandering energy in the delight at his total freedom.

Tiring at last, he concentrated on only one trail. He no longer wasted movement. He felt hollow inside and knew he had to find food while he still had enough strength to search.

The wind was rising. But without the driving snow, it worried him little. Still inept, he raced after some small animal. It disappeared under a huge fallen log partly visible above the snow.

Disappointed at losing his prey, feeling his hunger as a sharp pain inside, he sat down to chew the packed snow from the pads of his sore feet. It was then he saw, at the edge of a patch of bare ground, a rabbit like the one he'd chased yesterday.

Immediately, he was off. He raced against the wind. But his eagerness carried him past the spot where the rabbit had been sitting like a statue. His barking seemed to snap it into action. Inexperienced in the snow, Charlie couldn't stop. His front paws rammed deep into a drift. By the time he pulled them out, the rabbit had run.

A big black trap snapped on the animal when it darted under a bush. Charlie saw the rabbit writhing, and heard an agonized cry. Not wanting the thing to bite him as well, he moved forward with caution. The rabbit struggled for a short time. Then it lay still. Charlie nosed the dead animal. Food! At last.

His teeth closed on the rabbit's leg. Just then he heard a whiplike crack of something zinging past him. Startled, he leaped and ran. But the urgent need for food overcame his fear, and he turned back to the open place beneath the bushes. The wind carried the odor of the old man. The dog could hear him shout.

"You! Git! You ain't gonna rob my trap."

The man waved the gun in the air. When Charlie stood his ground, Caleb held the rifle to his shoulder, aiming. A bullet zinged over Charlie's head. The dog didn't know how the gun could hit from a distance, but he remembered the painful whack in the nose. It still hurt. Ignoring the rabbit, he ran.

He dodged through brush that scratched at his face, his only thought to put distance between him and the old man. Hunger burned, but his fear was stronger. He had never known people who punished. This new knowledge hurt in a way he had never been forced to feel before.

He lost all sense of direction, running without pause until the sun made long shadows, stretching from the trees. He no longer smelled the old man, nor could he hear the scolding voice. His stomach reminded him that he had eaten nothing that day but the few bits of meat clinging to his bone.

He noticed a spot of wetness in the snow. Another dog? The scent was similar. Was the other dog marking his territory? Then he saw some pellets on the whiteness. Their scent was like that of the rabbit. A little further on, he saw the rabbit. The wind was blowing toward it, and carried no odor of the little creature to him. The rabbit's nose twitched toward the cold wind, as if it were sniffing the air. In a flash, it darted toward a hole in the snow. The dog raced after it.

This time, he saw where it went. The hole angled down into a drift. Eagerly, he pushed his nose into the hole. The scent became stronger. He pulled back and started digging with his front paws. He would dig, then sniff, and dig again. He went deep into the snowdrift. Finally he reached hard earth.

There was a hole in it, too, but his paws scratched without making any dirt move. The scent urged him on, but there was nothing he could do. He couldn't make the entrance to the

rabbit's burrow in the frozen earth any bigger.
With a little bark of disappointment, he pulled
back out of the hole he had dug. The wind hit him
with all its freezing force.

There was a painful emptiness beneath his ribs.
Licking the snow from his muzzle, he became
aware of his burning thirst. There was a touch of
wetness on his tongue from the licking. He bit the
snow, and it made more wetness in his mouth.

As he was taking another big mouthful of snow,
a large animal emerged from behind a tree not far
away. It was at least as tall as he. The doglike
smell he had encountered earlier came to him
again. He was about to run toward the stranger
when he saw the rising hackles at the back of the
neck. He heard a throaty growl.

The two stood for a moment, studying each
other. Then, with a snarl of rage, the wolf sprang
toward him. Too weak to fight, Charlie turned and
ran for his life.

# 7

He knew the animal was nearing him. He could hear the sound of the wolf's heavy panting mingle with his own strained breathing. Fear gave him strength. He burst ahead and plunged over a drift. The heavy snow dragged at his legs.

He let out a terrified yelp as he felt the wolf's teeth grab a back paw. He yanked his leg free. The momentum carried him to a bare spot near a tree. Here, he could get better footing.

A small animal sprang up, pushing with its hind feet to dart out in front of him. He had startled it into fleeing. Tangling, they both fell. Charlie was on his feet again in an instant. Panic propelled him on through the forest.

The wolf veered off, chasing the rabbit as it skittered across the top of the drift. Charlie heard its thin cry and knew he was not being followed.

Still he ran, dodging boulders, spooked by the crack of a dead branch. Brush slapped his face and pulled at his shoulders. Every sound was a threat to his untrained ears. Would the wolf pick up his scent and pursue him again?

At last he had to stop. Wary, he faced the direction from which he had come, ready to leap away again if necessary. His thirst was overpowering. He dipped his head, taking mouthful after mouthful of snow. It eased the hurt in his middle, somewhat, and soothed the raw burn of his throat.

He must eat soon! He remembered the hamburger Maggie had shared with him yesterday. He hadn't really been hungry then. He had eaten more for the attention she gave.

Dark shadows and the rising moon told him it was time to go back to the shelter. Compared with the wolf's fangs, Betsy's wide teeth no longer seemed dangerous.

Though things were sharply outlined in the clear light of the moon, everything looked different. He had no idea which way to go. Strange cries distracted him. Hoots echoed from the tops of trees. A shriek sounded panic far away. A twig snapped nearby. Distant barking invited at the same time it frightened him. He wished he could see his own people, or some person who would protect him from these unknown dangers.

A huge bird swooped past him, lowering to the

31

snow, then rising in a great flap of wings. Something was caught in its claws, something that screamed like the rabbit in the trap.

A flash of home crossed his mind. He was tired and wanted his warm bed. Here, he was warm only when he ran. With clear skies, the temperature had dropped, and the wind blew colder.

Even more than shelter, he wanted something to eat. Moving by reflex, he nosed the ground for a hint of food, or a sign of the way back to the old man's cabin. He ran, sniffing as he went. Then he stopped, his ears alert. He turned them back and forth, trying to determine the source of the thud he had just heard.

He sniffed in a wide circle and found a bird that had fallen from a tree. It made a last feeble scratch with its frozen foot. Then it was still.

He picked it up in his mouth. His teeth crunched into its body. Saliva flowed. But his tongue was repelled by the roughness of the feathers. He spat it out. He pushed it with his nose, and bit it again. But a feather jabbed at the back of his throat. He could not eat it.

Discouraged, he blundered on. He slid, more than walked, down a slope. His strength was almost spent. He came to a long winding stream. He bent to drink at its bank, but his bruised nose touched something hard where water should have been. The moon only made everything more confusing.

There was no protection near the frozen creek. The wind hit him hard. He had to have shelter. He must sleep. Somehow he knew if he fell where he stood, he would never get up. It was too cold!

He threw back his head and howled. From a distance came an answering howl. He howled again, then remembered the wolf's frantic pursuit.

He remembered digging for the rabbit. He dug again, not knowing why. His ice-packed feet worked with a frenzy. Snow mounded up under his belly. He shoved it aside and continued digging. His paws were sore. Blood streaked the snow. He did not stop.

At last he made a burrow large enough to curl up in. He dropped. The last thing he saw before his eyes closed was a dark cloud drifting past the moon.

# 8

When Charlie awoke, he was completely covered. At first he thought Maggie had thrown a blanket over him. She played games like that. But when he raised his head, it emerged into the cold air of the mountain morning. He had been buried by snow that had fallen during the night. Stretching his stiff legs, he climbed out of his shelter.

His legs were shaky. Hunger had stolen his strength. It had been three days since he had eaten a complete meal. He labored back up the slope he'd slid down last night. Nose to the ground, he searched for anything that meant food. He was weak with the need of it. There were a few marks in the new snow, left by animals who had ventured out since last night's storm. He was not strong enough to chase, but when he found a scent, he followed it. Each ended in a hole in the snow.

A lone bird chirped defiant song. But sounds

were few, with the soft covering of new snow. Bare spots under bushes or beneath huge trees yielded a variety of odors. A white-footed mouse scurried away and disappeared at the base of a hollow tree.

Charlie pawed at the rotten wood, finding beetles in pupa stage, a layer under the bark. He devoured a mouthful encased in cocoons. He smelled the mouse and something else. Pawing deeper, he discovered the coiled body of a snake in hibernation under dead leaves and decaying wood. He ate it in two quick bites.

Continuing on at a slow pace, he paused to lift his head and listen. There was the snap of a dead branch, a distant voice.

He found the dead bird again. He didn't understand the cold stiffness of its body. But he had seen stiff bodies several times in the short while he'd been lost. Driven by hunger, he ate the bird, spitting out as many feathers as he could. Then he struggled on, his nose guiding him, always telling him where to go.

He caught a hint of the people smell, but it was not the old man. A little further on, he heard the crack of a rifle in the stillness. The noise threatened him.

He went on until a fence stopped him. On the other side, the smooth whiteness was unbroken except for a line of poles. He walked back and forth, looking for an opening in the fence. He found none.

He kept walking, still noticing the human odor now and then. There had been two men. He found where they had stood in the snow. Stumbling on, he finally discovered the faint but unmistakable scent of the mule. He followed it eagerly. When he broke into the clearing, he saw the cabin.

The old man was reaching something onto a small wooden platform almost hidden in the low branches of a cedar tree. Immediately, three or four little birds descended to the platform, chirping and pecking with energy. Charlie saw a bigger bird fly out of a tall pine. It dove down, cawing in a loud voice, and chased the other birds away.

"You blasted crow!" the old man shouted. "Those crumbs be for my sparrows."

He picked up a stick. Charlie shrank back behind a huge stump. But the old man threw the wood at the thieving crow. It cawed in raucous protest, but flew back to its roost in the pine tree. When the old man's back was turned, it came down once more. The smaller birds chattered with futile anger and flew away.

"Dang your feathers!"

The old man turned. He picked up the gun and pointed it at the crow. The rifle sounded. The crow flew away and did not return.

Not sure whether the man would point the gun at him, too, Charlie waited for him to disappear inside the cabin. Then he ran as fast as he could into the shelter at the back. He huddled in a far corner, away from the mule.

That animal set up an immediate fuss, braying at the top of its voice. Charlie bared his teeth and snarled. The stubborn animal only brayed louder, yanking its head up and down as it had done before.

"Betsy, quit your infernal racket. It be only a dog. I wouldn't let the critter stay if I thought he'd do you any harm."

The call came from the window of the cabin. Charlie saw the bearded face looking out the dirty window that faced the shed. He didn't understand the words, but the mule stopped its noise. She backed away from the dog into the other shielded corner. Her foot hit the bucket. Something splashed from it.

Charlie was thirsty! He approached the bucket, growling to warn the mule to keep her distance. For the first time since he had gotten lost, his tongue lapped water! Over and over it dipped into the bucket.

When his thirst was satisfied, he poked his nose into the big pan of cracked grain that the old man had supplied for the mule. It didn't smell good, or taste good, but he ate it anyway. It filled space in his stomach, but didn't satisfy his need for meat.

There were long shadows outside the shelter. He did not want to risk the hazards of another night in the forest. Here, at least, he had water, warmth, and safety.

# 9

As the days went by, Charlie came to know the ways of the forest. He was wary of the dangers it might conceal. He grew shrewd in his ability to find food. Rotting logs concealed insects or their larvae. Lizards and snakes hibernated there. He ate them all, his stomach dictating the need. He learned to survive.

He had been well fed before he got lost, and the extra layer of fat under his coat had allowed him time to make the mistakes of a newcomer to the wilderness. But the fat was gone. His skin now showed the line of his ribs, and hunger was almost constant. His inherent intelligence helped him to adjust. He'd had a life of ease, where everything had been provided. Now he faced the reality of eating grubs to stave off starvation.

Every day he tracked through the trees, even hunting down at the edge of the frozen stream. Sometimes he found an animal dead from the cold. These were times of feast, and he gorged himself against tomorrow's hunger. His teeth became expert at tearing apart a frozen body, gnawing and warming it enough to eat.

Hunger of another kind remained with him. He missed Maggie and her mother. He would have liked to hear the girl laugh while his tongue washed her face. Had the old man reached out a hand in friendship, he would have licked it joyfully.

The best he received from that source was an occasional knucklebone tossed carelessly at the base of a tree near the cabin. Each one he chewed bare of meat. Then he buried it.

One day he found a racoon in the bite of the black metal trap that had killed the rabbit. He recognized the smell of the old man on the metal and walked away. But the ever-present need for food forced him back. He could not resist fresh meat. Even when his stomach was full, he continued to chew on the carcass.

Zing! A rock flew past his head, landing with a thud a few inches away. He heard the old man shout.

"You ruined the fur, you useless cur! That hide would have brought in enough money to pay for a week's grub for me and Betsy!"

A hail of rock, ice chunks, and sticks pelted Charlie's thin body. He whirled and snarled, taking a few tentative steps toward his tormentor.

The gun had not sounded. He stood his ground. Then he saw the man level the rifle at him.

"I'll have your hide, you pesky trap-robber."

He braved the old man's wrath no longer. Dodging behind a boulder, he heard the cracking *cheeping* of the bullet striking the rock as he raced away through the forest.

Charlie did not venture near the cabin after that. Something in the memory of the angry voice kept him away. The nights were still cold, though the snow had begun to disappear. He sheltered where he could.

One night it rained, and he huddled under thick brush. The wetness from the sky continued to fall all the next day. At last he found a cave. He rushed in, shaking off the rain in spasms of shivering.

Wind was blowing rain in at the mouth of the cave. Charlie sniffed for danger, but the wind pushed any odors away from him. He could hear no sign of life in this sheltered place, so he moved farther back from the entrance. His eyes had not yet adjusted to the darkness, but his nose began to detect the evidence of another animal in the cave. Too cold and tired to think, he curled up to go to sleep. His back touched something that moved.

Alert again, he sprang to his feet, and whirled around. A mountain of fur seemed to be rolling

41

toward him. He edged back, never taking his gaze off the great creature. Then its roar rocked the walls of the cave! It was lumbering to a sitting position, moving slowly, as one still half asleep. Afraid to turn his back on the huge bear, Charlie continued to back toward the entrance. But when the bear reared to its feet and lunged, the dog whirled around and darted out of the cave. He was not fast enough to escape the raking swipe of the bear's paw.

"*Yi, yi, yi*," he cried, wanting to lick the pain in his torn leg, but afraid to stop.

The angry bear remained at the mouth of the cave, its body swaying back and forth. It roared its fury at being awakened too early.

Charlie ran through the driving rain, crashing through brush, dodging rocks, his feet skidding now and then in the thick pad of wet leaves under the trees. Not heeding the direction he had taken, he raced on. Above the timberline, he stopped on a ledge.

His ears told him some new danger was present: The whispering rattle of a pebble racing downward; an instinctual raising of the hair at the back of his neck; then it seemed that the mountain fell, burying him. The force of it toppled him off the ledge. He tumbled with rock and gravel, rolled by an energy he could not fight.

Downward! Downward! He could no longer tell

whether his feet were under him or not. His nose was clogged. He couldn't breathe!

As suddenly as it started, it stopped. Charlie felt himself lodged under all the debris. Even his head was covered. He panted and got a mouthful of dirt.

Crazed by the need for air, he thrust and pushed, but he could not move. He put all his strength into a great upward surge. He felt his nose break into free air. Another push, and he was able to lift his muzzle free. He gulped fresh air.

It came again, the rumble warning of disaster. Straining upward, he was able to force his whole head out. As he blinked the dirt from his eyes, he watched another avalanche thunder down the mountain. Small stones and dirt clods pelted his face. They hurt, but the pain was nothing compared with the panic at his inability to struggle free and run from this new and terrifying threat.

A tree snapped, and it was as if a gun had exploded in his ears. A boulder, loosened by the slide, hurtled past him. At last, silence came. Dirt and rocks stopped hitting him, but he was stunned.

Almost of themselves, his forelegs began to function. But frantic action only dug him deeper into the slide. He moved with deliberation. Strong survival instinct reasserted itself. Lifting and wriggling, he worked his front paws loose. Then, with a mighty effort, he pulled and dragged until his whole body stood clear on the mountainside. There was pain everywhere. But he could move. Too numb to leap over a tree that lay, newly fallen, in his path, he walked around it, going slowly downward.

The dirt he had breathed in choked him. He needed a drink. When the burbling sound of the stream reached his ears, he ran. He plunged his head into the water, then snapped it back with the shock of ice, barely melted. Gingerly, he drank. Splashing his head in and out of the water, he snorted to get the dirt out of his nostrils.

Then he dragged himself up the slope and followed the trail that led to the cabin. He limped into the mule's shelter. Let the old man come. Gun or no gun, he wanted to be dry, and safe from the mountain.

# 10

The rain had stopped. The sun was shining, and a whole new set of odors filled the air. The wind felt different, soft and friendly. Charlie stretched and arched his back at the entrance to the shelter.

Suddenly the old man darted past him. He picked up a pitchfork and lunged toward Charlie. Most of the dog's time in the mountains had been spent running from something. Now he stood his ground, snarling. In an angry hand, the pitchfork thrust toward him. But the man came no closer.

"Git, you dirty thief!" he rasped.

Charlie gave an answering growl. Neither advanced toward the other. But they did not retreat. Hostility crackled between them.

Betsy brayed. Caleb put down the fork and turned to her.

"Poor old girl. There you stand neglected, while this mangy critter defies me."

He stomped to the grain bin, lifted the lid, and

scooped out a bucketful of oats for the mule. Then he applied the pitchfork to the stale grass lining her corner, rearranging it.

"Nothing we can do for new bedding. That rain plumb soaked our whole stack."

He rubbed his hand along the mule's neck.

"We'll get you out to stretch your legs right soon. Have to traipse into town soon as you're limbered up proper."

He backed around Charlie at the entrance, snorting, "Maybe I didn't have the heart to jab your skinny bones this time. But don't be getting any ideas."

The warmth of the spring day brought back a scent the dog remembered, and that other hunger, the wanting of a friendly touch, returned. He whined, but the old man only glared as he strode away.

"No, sir. Don't think I forgot about that trap you robbed. No way at all."

Left with no one but Betsy for company, Charlie fell to licking the place where the bear's paw had raked his leg. Then he limped off in search of a meal. He had learned to move on silent feet, and often came upon animals feeding. His hunting had improved. Today he ate.

His curious nose encountered other things. Deer antlers, like bony branches of a strange tree, lay in his path. He sniffed them. They smelled of animal. He gnawed at them to see what they were made of, but discarded them. They seemed like very stale bones. He meandered on, enjoying the new season.

Stopping under a dogwood tree, white with bloom, he caught sight of a tall animal with ears like Betsy's. He looked in wonder at the branch-like bones rising above its ears. They were fastened to its head and moved as the head turned. The deer stood still as a stone. A gun cracked, and it leaped out of sight.

Loneliness turned Charlie back to the shelter. There, he had at least shared warmth with the mule on cold nights. Near the cabin, he watched a pair of squirrels rolling and tumbling at play. Some of his puppy zeal returned.

He bounded in at the mule and surprised her lying down. He had never seen her down before. She seemed more his size, like someone to romp with.

When he charged at her, uttering a yap that was meant to say, "Let's scuffle," she threw up her head, rolling her eyes. She struggled to her feet and backed away. Charlie still wanted to tussle, and he nipped her playfully. She jumped around and turned to aim a kick at him. It missed, but there was no fun in that! He gave up and went to lie down in his corner.

He was still there when Caleb came in to put

leather straps over Betsy's head and fit something into her mouth. His creaking old voice seemed to have caught the spirit of spring, and he was singing a tuneless song.

"Oh, do you remember sweet Betsy from Pike? She crossed the high mountain . . ."

The song broke off as he started pulling at the reins, urging the mule out into the sunlight of mid-morning. He paid no attention to the dog's wistful glance.

"Come on. Gotta get those old legs loosened up. Time to get down and stock up on supplies for the summer, before them pesky tourists come packin' into town."

He was chuckling to himself. He took an old straw hat out of the rafters, settling it over Betsy's ears at a cockeyed angle.

"We'll even keep the sun out of your eyes. You've been caged up in here so long, you're no doubt blind in the daylight."

The mule stumbled. Charlie got to his feet, wary of being kicked at again. The mule recovered and took a few more steps. Then she slipped on a rock. She dropped to her front knees, with her rump still high. For a dog, this would be a morning stretch, but pain sounded in the noise she made, so much thinner than her usual irritating bray. The old man stooped beside her. He slipped his arms under her chest and tried to lift her.

The dog's breeding told him to help. He bounded toward Betsy, nipping gently at her face much as he had done earlier in play. She scrambled up with such energy she toppled the old man backward. He lay in the pine needles looking from mule to dog, scratching his beard.

"I do declare. First good thing that ornery dog ever done!"

Charlie wagged his tail as if he knew it had been a good thing, and he deserved petting. But Caleb ignored him. Later, however, Charlie found a fresh bone with plenty of meat clinging to it. And the old man sat on the front step and watched while the dog chewed it.

# 11

Guns continued to boom in the forest in the days that followed. Daily, as Charlie hunted, he came upon the human scent. There were always two men together, and he found places where they skinned and gutted their kill. He ate of their leavings.

Once he heard the old man muttering to himself.

"Danged poachers! Ain't nowhere near deer season. Bet my life they'll be selling that meat. If I had a chance, I'd put the law on them, sure enough."

The words meant nothing to the dog. And the old man always turned his attention to the mule. Charlie lingered sometimes, hoping for another chance to earn a word of grudging praise. Now that starvation was no longer his main concern, he yearned for companionship.

Each day the mule was led out for a walk. Each day they went further. Charlie often followed. The dry air was becoming hot. One day Caleb led

Betsy down to the stream. At the water's edge, he stopped to take off his shoes. He rolled up his pant legs and stepped into the water. Holding Betsy's reins, he coaxed the mule a little way into the brook. He splashed water on her sides and scrubbed her skin.

Charlie splashed in upstream from them. The water was still cold, but it no longer held the icy shock he had experienced after the avalanche.

Ducks landed on the stream. They quacked occasionally as they glided over the water. Charlie hadn't seen ducks on the water. He watched them skim along without seeming to push themselves. One flipped its head and neck under the water, its rear lifting. Webbed yellow feet flapped. Another plunged its head into the water and came up with a morsel of food in its bill.

The mule dipped her head. She smacked the water with her nose, splashing the old man. Caleb laughed. Charlie drank deeply, then edged nearer the man. He wanted to be part of the fun, not just a bystander.

Betsy turned and scrambled out onto the rocky bank. Caleb followed, chuckling and patting the mule, encouraging her up to level footing. He looked happier than the dog had ever seen him, and his grumpiness was gone.

Suddenly, the mule kicked with a hind leg. She caught Charlie off guard and knocked him rolling.

The old man slapped his leg and roared with laughter.

"That's my Betsy. Plenty of pepper in you yet."

There were no comforting sounds for the dog. He wasn't hurt, but his dignity was wounded. The old man had laughed at him. Betsy and Caleb were friends. Charlie was clearly an outsider. He slunk away.

# 12

The dog wandered aimlessly along the familiar path, heading toward the shelter. He wanted a home! He wanted a friend. He would have to go elsewhere to find them.

He turned deep into the forest, catching the scent of a mule. It wasn't Betsy. He sniffed the human odor. The hunters he had known about all winter. He started following their trail. The need for companionship was a strong pain inside.

He came to a fence and saw the asphalt road. A memory flashed through his thoughts. He remembered the day he had gotten lost in the mountains. He thought of Maggie, who had loved him. He remembered the gentle touch of her mother's hand.

He barked out a greeting as a car approached. But it sped past, children shouting to him from the open car window. He waited by the road, not feeling any particular hope. He just waited. At last he gave up, and began following the scent of a rabbit.

Wandering into a clearing where the grass had grown almost as high as his head, he saw a pair of deer. One had branching antlers. Between the pair, barely visible in the tall grass, was a fawn. They were there for an instant. A sound came from nearby, and they disappeared. From the trees came an angry voice.

"Spook my deer, will you!"

The only human voice he'd heard in months, except for the old man's. And it sounded mean! No friendship here. The ache inside grew larger, and Charlie turned away.

Then came the cracking sound of a rifle shot, and almost at the same time, a burning pain in his right shoulder! It was so intense the leg folded under him and he fell, howling with despair and fear.

"Jerk, that was a dog you hit!"

"I meant to."

"He had nothing to do with the deer. They just went."

"Outa the way. You're spoiling my aim."

The voices reached Charlie through a haze of pain. He could not tell what was going on around him. He was dimly aware of the man's rage being directed at him, and knew he should run away. But his attempt to get up was futile. He lay helpless under a scrubby bush, his entire body shaking with the pain. His leg seemed almost disconnected from his body. Even if he did succeed in getting up, he couldn't run.

"Come on, Buck. No sense hanging around here."

"I'm just going to finish the job."

"You're not killing that dog!"

"None of your business what I do."

The men's angry voices terrified Charlie. Then a third voice cut into their argument.

"Git!"

The dog barely recognized the old man's shout. He did not dare hope for help from him. There was a sudden loud braying. A strange mule bolted out from the trees. Charlie registered the only protest he could muster against the threat of being trampled or kicked. He gave a feeble yip. The animal shied and veered away from the dog, spilling its load as it jumped over a log and escaped. One of the hunters ran after the frightened mule, calling "Whoa, boy. Easy there."

"You did that on purpose, you crazy old coot!" the remaining man yelled. "You stampeded my mule. Now I've got to — "

The old man's voice cut in.

"Git!"

The poacher swore and spun around, peering through the trees.

"It's public land. You can't order me around."

"Land's for them as uses it proper. Poaching be illegal. Now git!"

The hunter continued to search the forest with a shifting gaze. His partner came back empty-handed.

"Might as well pack it in. Our mule's halfway down the mountain by now." He shouldered his rifle and picked up his gear. The other man snorted.

"I'm not leaving. That old hermit isn't going to think he can scare me off."

He was left talking to himself as the other man shrugged and strode away. Seeing that he was being left, the poacher swore and kicked a rotten stump.

"Chicken. Run with your tail between your legs. See if I care."

To punctuate the words, he fired into the air. Charlie cringed. The sound of a pump-action shotgun issued an ominous warning in the stillness that followed the shot.

"I ain't much for words. Now git!"

The old man's voice did not crack or quaver. The poacher clenched his teeth. He crouched, rifle readied, looking about to locate a target. The old man's shotgun roared, cutting down a shower of leaves and twigs. *Tchuk-tuk-klnk*. The pump sounded again. With one last vengeful kick at the stump, the poacher grabbed his gear.

"You haven't heard the last of this," he sputtered.

He slouched away in the direction his partner had taken. His voice could be heard muttering curses as he stomped off. Silence settled over Charlie, who was too numb to care what might happen.

Moments passed. The natural whispers, caws, and screeches of the forest returned to signal safety. The old man stumbled over a fallen log to reach the dog. Charlie could feel himself being lifted gently. He could hardly hear the thin, cracking voice that said, "Side-winding varmint! *My* dog he shot."

Even in his stupor, the dog felt a warm breath of hope.

# 13

When Charlie gained consciousness, he was lying in his usual corner of the shed. From inside the cabin, he heard the old man singing.

". . . tall Shanghai rooster and a big yaller dog."

The dog struggled to rise. His right shoulder and leg were held stiff, tied to a piece of wood. Not understanding, he reared up, only to fall back. Almost immediately, he tried again. The pain shooting down his leg reminded him of the hunter's gun.

"Lie still, you scruffy beast! You'll ruin all my work to put that shoulder back together."

The old man ran to kneel beside Charlie, pushing him down and holding him there. The voice was rough, as it had always been, but the hands did not hurt him.

"Rest easy for a few days. It'll mend just fine."

Caleb cupped his hands and brought some water to the dog's mouth. Charlie, exhausted from trying to get to his feet, let the water trickle over his tongue. His head fell back onto the straw cushioning his body, and his eyes drooped shut. He slept.

Later, he lifted his head. Caleb's hands were there, giving him water. Even the effort to lap his tongue into the cupped hands tired him. Again he slept.

Time meant nothing to him. He knew neither day nor night. He simply drifted, sometimes getting water from gentle hands, sometimes hearing the mule and whining in fear of being kicked. He would have fought against this helplessness, but sleep always came to soothe him.

At last he wakened to hear the howl of a wolf far away. It was dark. Sleeping most of the time, he had forgotten the stiffness of his right leg. He wanted to hunt. Hunger was sharp in his stomach, and his senses were finally alert.

But when he tried to get up, the stick on his leg made a struggle for him. He became angry. He strained his neck and chewed at the wood and cloth holding his leg. When it would not come loose, he howled in frustration.

"What in tarnation?"

The old man stood before him, glowering.

"A man can't git a decent night's sleep no more!"

When Caleb's hands reached down to him,

Charlie snarled. He had heard anger before and expected pain from that anger.

"I ain't planning to do you damage. I 'spect you're hungry, dad-burn you. But that ain't no call to yowl at me!"

Caleb put something near Charlie, and he let his hand hover for a moment over the dog's head. Abruptly, he straightened and stomped away.

Charlie smelled meat! He wriggled and squirmed until his nose touched the food. An extra push, and his teeth grasped it. He wolfed it down.

Eating awakened an almost overpowering thirst. The faint light of dawn marked the outlines of the shed. He saw the mule, legs folded to her chest, lying down with her eyes closed. Good. If she were sleeping standing up, as she often did, she'd be more likely to kick or stomp him when she opened her eyes.

He worked and struggled, pushing with his good left foreleg, and finally managed to get his hind legs under him. With a last awkward surge, he stood on three feet. The hated stick held his fourth out at an angle from his body. Twinges of pain stabbed in the wounded shoulder. But he was standing, and the hurt grew no worse.

Unsteady from lying down so long, and weakened by not having eaten for several days, he staggered and lunged about the shelter. He finally located a bowl of water, placed near the folded coat that had lately pillowed his head.

The stiff piece of wood made it difficult to lower his head to the bowl, but he persisted. When his tongue found the cool water, his anger died. He drank his fill and toppled nearby to sleep again, worn out by his efforts.

The sun, reaching through the entrance, was hot when Charlie awoke. The old man crouched beside him. The wooden splint was no longer tied to his leg. Caleb examined the shoulder, hurting a little as he probed. Charlie's lip curled back to snarl, then stopped. The hands moved away, and the pain eased. The old man *had* helped him. Maybe he was a friend, after all.

"It'll heal by itself now, if you're willin' to take it easy a few more days."

A hand dropped to Charlie's head and patted it. He made a happy little noise. The hand drew back and searched out something lying in the straw.

"Hmph. Reckon I took this off of you when I patched your shoulder."

The old man harrumphed, as if trying to clear something out of his throat.

"Wasn't paying it no mind then. Guess I just flung it over here."

There was silence. Charlie lifted his head, hoping to be petted again. The old man studied the engraved brass plate that lay flat against the strap of leather.

"Hmph!"

Charlie looked up into the old man's face. The mouth, almost hidden by the thick beard, was set in a straight line.

"Duke Charlemagne von Arnhausen. Fancy name. Fancy dog."

A deep sigh escaped Caleb's tight lips.

"Not for such as me."

The collar dangled in one hand as he crouched to put a pan of food near the dog. Charlie's tongue licked his hand before he drew it away.

"Quit that! I ain't getting friendly with the likes of you."

He shook the collar in his clenched fist.

"You ain't my dog. It says here who you belong to."

He threw the collar across the shelter and stomped out, kicking Betsy's water bucket as he went.

After that, meat and water were there in plenty whenever Charlie awakened. But, though the man tended to the mule regularly and patted her with as much affection as ever, he never came near the dog when Charlie was awake.

Each day, Charlie was able to move a little further, and with less effort. One morning he followed the old man out of the shed. Caleb stopped, and Charlie caught up to him. But when the dog licked the man's hand, it yanked away.

"Git, now! None of that."

Charlie cried softly. A dull ache settled back in its familiar place somewhere under his ribs. He did not see the longing gaze that followed him as he limped away under the pines.

# 14

Charlie wanted to run. He needed the sense of freedom that had drawn him into the wilderness months ago, but his muscles were weakened by the inactivity of the last several weeks. And there was still pain and stiffness in the hurt shoulder.

Dispirited, he wandered. The sun rose high overhead. He found the fence and the road that had brought him to the mountains. He didn't have the strength to leap over the gate as he had done then. A dim memory of his people came to him again.

A car approached. He became alert. But the car only slowed while its occupant threw out a bottle. It struck a fencepost and shattered. The car sped on.

Charlie sat with his nose pressed between the bars of the gate for a long time. Finally, his hunger urged him to search for food. Turning, he began to sniff the trails crisscrossing before him. He recognized the scent of a rabbit. He tried to hurry after it. But it was no use. The stiff leg made him walk like an old man with a cane.

He saw the rabbit sitting under a low-hanging branch of a thorny bush. He froze. The rabbit's mouth continued to move in a chewing motion. No way to sneak up on it, even though the wind was blowing toward Charlie. His dragging leg made too much noise when he moved.

With a little whine, he stumbled toward a fallen tree. In its rotted log, he might find something to eat. But his injury made it hard to paw at the wood. When his teeth tore at the looser parts, he found nothing but a few dry cocoons, empty of nourishment. The season for larvae and hibernating snakes was past.

Days of hunger threatened again. He forgot everything but the food at the old man's shelter. He managed a stiff-legged gait that was faster than walking. He hurried, panting in the heat. It was exhausting. How long he hobbled, he didn't know. His lungs were almost bursting with the effort. He wanted to drop. Pausing, he eased the throb in his shoulder for a moment. Finally, he folded his right paw back, and ran on three legs.

He heard a mule hee-hawing. He caught the strong scent of the animal. Betsy! He must be close to the cabin.

It was easier to move through the forest on

three legs. He gained skill with his three-legged pace as he hurried on. It seemed a long time before he broke into the clearing. He stopped. There was a sense of something different.

Nearing the cabin, he saw nothing unusual, except that the door stood open. He heard a sound.

Wary, he rounded the corner and rushed into the shed. To his surprise, Betsy was not in her corner. She was not in the shelter at all.

He caught the hated scent of the poacher who had shot him. He heard another sound from the cabin, a low moan. It was louder this time. He barked.

"Dog!"

Hesitant, he walked slowly to the open door at the front of the cabin. He put his nose inside. He remembered the first time he had attempted to go through this doorway. The stick had whacked his nose. He turned away, but stopped when he heard another moan.

"Dog!"

The old man's voice did not have its customary gruffness.

"Help me, dog."

When Charlie ventured inside, he saw the old man lying on the floor. Going nearer, he smelled blood.

He began licking where blood had thickened in the matted hair at the back of the man's head.

For a while, Caleb said nothing. At last he forced himself to a sitting position.

"Cussed sidewinder! Whacked me a good one!"

Charlie stood back, still uncertain. Caleb struggled onto his hands and knees. He remained thus for a while, shaking his head as if to clear it. He moaned softly to himself. Then, with obvious effort, he stood up.

"Betsy?"

He stumbled to the window at the back and peered out. His hands clenched into fists. A roar of anger came. Charlie backed away toward the door. Torn between hunger and fear, he paced back and forth near the entrance. The man's anger had hurt him before.

"He took my Betsy!"

His voice registered disbelief. The dog saw him slump onto the bed. His head dropped into his hands. His shoulders shook.

"If he done anything to harm her . . ."

Caleb lapsed into silence. Charlie felt an urge to comfort the man, and he edged closer. His stiff leg rasped on the rough floor. He stopped. His overtures of friendship had been pushed away before.

He took another step and stopped. His leg dragged. A step. Stop. Another step. At last, hearing sad sounds, Charlie timidly put his chin on Caleb's knee.

# 15

Shadows darkened the room. Charlie no longer heard noises from the old man, but his own stomach growled. He turned to limp to the door.

"Where you going, pup?"

The sound was quiet, not gruff. Looking back, the dog whined and licked his nose.

"Well, Mr. Duke Charlemagne von . . . whatever your name might be . . ."

Silence followed, punctuated by deep sighs from the old man and another small whine from the dog.

"Whoever gave you the collar ain't here."

In the quiet of the dark room, Charlie's stomach rumbled, telling his hunger. The man stood, moving as if he had aged a great deal. He lit a kerosene lamp, turning the wick down as the lamp started to smoke from a high, flickering flame. He took some dried strips of venison from a cupboard and tossed them toward the dog.

"I 'spect Betsy'll be wanting some grain."

Caleb's drooping shoulders shook, and his groan seemed to come from his whole body.

"I forgot. She's gone."

Charlie gobbled the jerky so fast he almost didn't feel it going down his throat. He needed more, and he was thirsty. But he did not venture near the old man staring out the back window. Suddenly, as if a decision had been made, the man squared his shoulders and turned to the dog.

"Maybe you *are* somebody else's dog. A body careless enough to lose you in these wilds."

He strode out of the cabin with purpose. Charlie followed. The man entered the shed and got down on his hands and knees to search through the straw. The dog found the water bowl and drank deeply.

The old man stood up, triumphantly waving the dog's collar. Charlie backed away, expecting another angry outburst.

"Somebody else's dog don't mean you can't help me. Your nose can tell me where he took my Betsy."

The old man shook the collar, as if to emphasize a thought.

"Maybe that somebody don't have any idea where you was lost. Maybe you won't be needing this no more!"

Caleb scratched his beard. "Leastways, ain't nobody going to find this here contraption by mistake."

He stuffed the collar deep into his pants pocket. As he went to Charlie, he held out his hand with the palm up. Doubtfully, the dog touched it with his nose. For the first time, the hand genuinely patted Charlie. The love that had been bottled up in the dog's aching chest exploded. He licked the hand with a frenzy of affection. He jumped up and tried to lick the man's face. He barked. The mouth he had carried in a straight line all this time curved up in a smile, matching the smile on Caleb's face.

There was no anger in the man's voice when he spoke. It was rich with a feeling that Charlie couldn't identify.

"Cut that out. A person could get used to it. Might even learn to like it."

Then, with urgency pushing out emotion, the voice ordered, "You take me where they went. Help me find where that varmint took my Betsy."

The man grabbed his rifle, hesitated, and put it aside in favor of the sturdier shotgun leaning against the wall.

"Be more gumption to a shotgun," he said.

Charlie, knowing something was expected of him, leaped about as well as he could on three legs. He pawed at the old man's pantleg, barking.

"Shhh!" You be quiet now."

Caleb's hands pushed Charlie's nose to the ground, and he repeated "Betsy, Betsy."

Charlie understood. He circled, sniffed the ground, and picked up the mule's scent crossing the clearing. It was pitch black as he started following the trail. Behind him, the old man sputtered. "You might wait for a body." He flashed on the dim light of a flashlight. Charlie saw the old man stumble, as if he did not know the area. Yipping softly, the dog went to him. Caleb's hand rested on Charlie's head.

"Good boy!"

Through the night, there were no other words of praise. The man said nothing. Charlie didn't need words now. He knew he was needed. He could take the old man to find his mule.

The dog developed a loping, three-footed confidence, curving his right paw high enough to clear entangling vines and fallen branches. His superior night vision told him where each rock was and how to avoid burrows and mounds of dirt left by the burrowers.

An owl swooped low, made a catch, and flapped high into a tree, advertising its victory with a *"Hoo, hoot."*

"Wha . . . ?" the old man exclaimed. A twisting branch underfoot had tripped him. Instantly, Charlie was at his side. When he was assured that the man was on his feet again, the dog forged

71

ahead. They passed over a river bed layered with rocks and mud. Concentrating, Charlie splashed through the trickle of water remaining at the middle of the river. He found the trail beyond. Where was Caleb?

He backtracked and found the man lying flat at the water's edge, sputtering under his breath. Each time he tried to get up, he slipped in the wetness and fell back. The dog nudged him and yipped a soft encouragement. He allowed the man to brace a hand on the fur of his back. When Caleb was standing on his own, Charlie hurried to find the scent again. He was ready to go on when he heard an urgent whisper.

"Sssst! Help a man over these consarned rocks."

He returned again, and this time he walked beside Caleb until they gained surer footing. The first hint of light touched the sky.

At last, Charlie broke out of the dense forest onto a wider, more traveled path. It was a firebreak cut through the forest. He spotted a cabin nestled under some giant oak trees and cedar. The scent of mule was stronger. Where was the old man?

Again he went back. The man's foot had dropped into a hole. He was trying to pull his leg out. Charlie pushed Caleb's hands aside with his nose. He grasped the pant leg with his teeth and pulled. A moan of pain slipped through the man's grinding teeth.

"I ain't good for nothing anymore."

He rubbed his ankle. Charlie tugged at his shirt-sleeve. Caleb struggled to his feet, steadying himself with a hand on the dog's back. He reeled, almost falling.

"Guess that crack he gave me on the noggin done more damage than I thought."

Charlie waited. Caleb leaned against a nearby tree. The sun reddened the eastern sky before he was ready to go on. Birds chirped and flitted from branch to branch, tree to tree. A squirrel scolded, then scurried farther up the trunk of an ancient cedar, its bushy tail curling up over its back. Charlie nudged the old man.

"Yeah, I know. Time we be getting on our way."

The dog led the way. When they came out onto the firebreak, he made a tiny sound, pointing his nose toward the cabin.

"Sssst!" the man whispered.

Together they approached the tumbledown hut from the back. There, securely tied to a scrubby oak, was Betsy. She appeared unharmed, and not in the least disturbed by the other mule tethered beside her.

When she recognized the old man, she set up a braying caterwaul that might have wakened the entire forest. Swearing under his breath, Caleb hurried to her. He leaned his shotgun against the tree and closed her huge mouth with both his hands. As he did so, he pressed his face against hers.

Watching, Charlie felt deserted again. The old man had his mule and seemed to have forgotten all else. A dog was no longer needed. He slipped behind a nearby boulder, prepared to leave them. He stopped for a last backward glance.

Just then the poacher came around the corner. Charlie's head lifted. A growl of hate came from deep in his throat. Warned, the old man made a dive for his shotgun. He was too late. The poacher already had the gun leveled at Caleb's head. Charlie tensed, silent.

"You're getting to be a pest," the poacher grunted. "Guess I'll have to get rid of you. Maybe in a ravine, under a landslide."

Betsy brayed.

"Shut up, mule," he said. "If this old goat had kept his nose out of my business, he'd be safe up in the hills."

*Tchuk-tuk-klnk.*

The threatening sound of the pump action triggered Charlie into action. His hackles rose. He had heard that sound before, after he was hurt. Three legs or not, he moved as if his life depended on his speed. Before the poacher had time to take in what was happening, he sprang.

74

*"Arruarrugh!"*

The dog acted on pure instinct. The impact of his leap knocked his enemy down. The gun fell from his hands, discharging with a mighty *ka-boom!* Glaring anger, Charlie drew back his lips, baring his teeth. Gripping the man's throat, he clenched his jaws. The poacher wriggled beneath him, trying to get away. He flailed with both arms, and tried to get a leg up to kick the dog away. Charlie only tightened his grip on the throat.

The old man grabbed the gun, reloaded, and pointed it at the poacher.

"You can let him go now."

Charlie did not loosen his jaws. Approaching with caution, Caleb put his hand on the dog's head.

"You can let the slimy critter up now."

When Charlie still did not respond, the old man tugged at his good shoulder. A garbled plea squeaked from the fallen man. His hands pushed. The old man tugged.

Finally, Charlie backed off, snarling. He stood eyeing the man who had shot him. This person had hurt the old man and stolen the mule. Charlie did not understand why he had to let him go.

The poacher sat up, grasping his neck. A small trickle of blood oozed between his fingers. He began sliding backward on his rump over the rough gravel.

"Hold it!" the old man commanded.

75

Charlie took a tentative step in the poacher's direction, his teeth bared. The man gave a terrified cry. Groveling, he whined, "Keep your dog off me! He'll kill me."

The old man snorted with disgust.

"You left him to die. What you expect?"

Then, tying Betsy to the tree again, the old man waved the poacher to his feet.

"Don't try nothing. You start to run, and the dog'll be right after you."

Charlie remained by the old man's side as the three of them entered the cabin door.

"You got a phone! One of them contraptions you can ring up the sheriff on?"

The poacher gestured to the telephone standing on an old crate near the window.

"Use it!"

The poacher started to bluster about how he'd be glad to get the sheriff to arrest the old man and his killer dog.

"Use it!"

The poacher edged toward the door. Charlie moved to block his escape.

"*Rrrr*," he warned, the fur standing up at the back of his neck.

Caleb gestured with the gun, pointing to the phone.

"Get Sheriff Alderman. When he gets here, you can tell him anything you want. But I'm guessin' you got things here you don't want him to see. We'll see who gets arrested."

Reluctantly, the poacher picked up the phone and dialed. After the call had been made, Charlie settled himself in front of the door. His eyes did not leave the poacher, who was slumped in the chair by the phone. He didn't understand the old man's way of dealing with this. Humans had strange ways. But he made sure the poacher could not leave.

# 16

As time went on, Charlie felt the drain of a day spent limping through the forest, and the strain of the night trailing Betsy. His head drooped onto his front paws. The poacher's chair made a noise as he shifted. At once the dog's head lifted. He saw Caleb's shoulders drooping. He watched the bearded head nod and the old man's eyes close. The head snapped up with a jerk, and Caleb was alert again.

The man they watched grew restless. He squirmed, moving one foot, then the other. Outside, all the forest inhabitants had silenced in the noonday sun. Heat combined with fatigue to make Charlie drowsy. But he would not sleep. Without knowing the reason, he waited. Then a motor could be heard. Tires crunched on the gravel outside.

"In here, Sheriff!" the old man bellowed. He got

up and stomped to the door. "We treed you a skunk!"

A tall man in uniform entered, laughing.

"What's gotten into you, Caleb? Skunks don't climb trees."

Charlie stood, barking. He sniffed the sheriff's pant leg. The man reached out his hand, allowing Charlie to smell that he was not an enemy.

Caleb grunted. "Maybe you're right. This critter rightly belongs under a rock, or in a hole in the ground."

When the sheriff approached the poacher, Charlie walked between them, as if to make sure no one let the man go. A growl rumbled in his throat.

"Dog!" the old man said.

"It's OK, boy," the sheriff said in an easy voice. "I just want to see who you've got here."

He scratched the back of Charlie's neck before he tilted the poacher's averted face around so he could study it.

"Buck Aimsley! I thought they still had you down in the reformatory."

The sheriff pushed back his hat and wiped sweat from his forehead.

"I guess that was a few years back. What devilment have you been up to lately?"

"Make the dog go away," the poacher pleaded.

"He ain't likely to budge," Caleb snorted. "Looks like he's taken a fancy to you."

The young man pulled back his collar and pointed to the teeth marks and dried blood on his neck.

"See what his dog did to me."

The old man sputtered, "Served the varmint right."

"They came gunning for me, Sheriff. I tell you, that old coot's crazy. He almost let his dog kill me."

"Was his own doing, Sheriff."

"And they broke into my cabin. You have to arrest them."

"Dang it, Sheriff. If you'll just listen to me a minute — "

"He's got nothing to tell!"

Old Caleb's face puffed with frustration. He grabbed a frying pan from the nearby stove and slammed it to the floor.

"I ain't much with words, Sheriff Alderman, but dang it, that sidewinder stole my mule!"

The sheriff grinned with mischief.

"You mean that old fleabag you drag into town with you just so she can tote home your load of supplies?"

At that the old man's anger reached a new height. But he drew himself up with dignity.

"Betsy be the finest animal ever to come down the pike," he said. "If you can't respect — "

"Just pulling your leg, Caleb," the sheriff said, still grinning. Then his face straightened. "This sounds like nothing more than a kid's prank. I agree, he's old enough to know better. But if I know the judge, it's not likely Buck'll even get a night in jail for it."

"If she were your animal . . ."

At that moment, Betsy brayed. Glancing out the open window, the sheriff observed, "Looks like you've got her back." He wiped his forehead again, looking disgruntled. "Was it worth calling me all the way up here on a hot day like this?"

"That ain't all the skunk done. Shot the dog, he did, and — "

The poacher interrupted. "That was an accident."

"Then why'd your friend walk out on you?"

"Look, you two. I don't intend to spend my time listening to the pair of you argue."

The sheriff walked to the door.

"Buck, from now on, leave mules alone."

"I've got a good mind to swear out a complaint on the old jerk and his dog. They almost killed me."

"Caleb?"

"He called it on hisself," Caleb sputtered.

The sheriff looked at Charlie. "What's your story, buddy? I think you could explain everything a lot more clearly, if only you could talk."

Charlie was tired. He wanted a drink, he wanted rest, and he wanted the friendship he heard in the sheriff's voice. He limped toward the outstretched hand and put his chin in it.

"Always had that limp, old fellow?"

The poacher stood and edged nearer the window. He put a hand on the windowsill.

Caleb said, "I been trying to tell you . . ."

He jerked a thumb toward the poacher.

"He shot the dog deliberate. Claimed the dog spooked his deer."

"You crazy old polecat!"

"Yep, shot him apurpose. Woulda finished him off, too, but his friend wouldn't hear of it. Then I stopped him."

"Don't listen to him, sheriff. He imagines all that stuff. He's just trying to get out of my signing a complaint."

The sheriff grasped Buck Aimsley by the shoulder and pushed him back into the chair.

"You'll get a chance to talk. But I'm going to hear you out one at a time. You first, Caleb."

"He's just going to tell you a bunch of lies, Sheriff."

"Shut up! One more word out of you, Buck, and

I'll run you in for disturbing the peace. My peace of mind!"

He pointed to the seated man and directed Charlie to watch him. Drooping with fatigue, Charlie obliged.

"OK, Caleb. Let me hear the whole story, deer and all."

Without distractions, Caleb was able to make a full report in short order.

"I'm guessing they got a freezer around here someplace. And you'll be finding hides from the last kill, too."

It didn't take long to discover a false wall concealing a huge freezer.

"Venison in it, enough to give the whole town a big feed. They was a trifle slow getting this last batch to where they sell it, I guess."

Grim-faced, Sheriff Alderman handcuffed the poacher and led him to the four-wheel drive squad car.

"You've got no proof. I was just here for the night," Buck protested.

A stern glance from the sheriff silenced him.

Following everyone outside, Charlie curled up around the coolness of a shaded rock and immediately fell asleep. Caleb settled himself on the rock and closed his eyes.

The motor purred into action. Tires crunched

on gravel and twigs as the car backed around. Suddenly, without stopping the engine, the sheriff put the car in neutral, slid from behind the wheel, and walked over to face Caleb.

"When did you get that dog, Caleb?"

Caleb's head sagged, and he made a slight snoring sound.

"Caleb!"

The old man's eyes opened. He lifted his head and blinked.

"The dog, Caleb? Where'd you get him?"

"I told you. He got hisself shot. Weren't no one else to care for him."

"So you just found him?"

"Might could say that."

The sheriff cleared his throat and kicked a dead branch.

"A woman and her daughter reported a shepherd lost in the big blizzard last October."

"Mighty poor time to be losing a critter. It maybe died."

"Yes, it might have. Or it might be this German shepherd, the one you found."

Caleb took a long time to respond.

"Might could be they forgot about it. Maybe even got theirselves another dog."

"They just got back from Hawaii, where the mother was working. Called last week, hoping I'd heard something."

He looked directly into Caleb's eyes. "It's the girl's dog, really. She was pretty sad about losing him." He paused. "She's a nice kid, Caleb."

Caleb blinked again. Without another word, he rammed his hand into his pocket and pulled out the collar. Charlie shifted in his sleep, but did not waken.

# 17

Charlie slept a long time. The last two days had been demanding, and he hadn't had time to rebuild his strength. When he awoke, he felt ravenous.

"Well, now. Sleeping Beauty! Or I might could call you Rip Van Winkle."

The old man stood at the door of the poacher's cabin. A delicious aroma wafted out. Charlie didn't wait to do his usual stretching. He didn't stop to see whether the old man was in one of his rare agreeable moods. Stumbling to his feet, he charged up the two steps and through the door. He yipped and put his good front paw on the edge of the table from which the good smell came. Unable to reach the plate of cooked venison, he barked with impatience.

"Keep your shirt on, Buster!"

The old man walked to the table. He seemed preoccupied. When he sat down and made no move to feed Charlie, the dog pushed at his hand with a demanding nose. Absentmindedly, the hand began to scratch behind the dog's ears.

"Can't keep on calling you Buster. Reckon they called you Duke?"

Charlie wanted to eat. He pulled back his head and pawed at the old man's knee.

"Don't sound right, nohow. Duke? Naw. Charlemagne?"

Giving up, Charlie walked slowly toward the open door. If the old man would not feed him, he would have to forage for himself.

"Charlie? Reckon they made it Charlie?"

Hearing the name his people had called him, the dog turned and made a lonely sound.

"That be it. Charlie! Here, Charlie. Come here, boy."

If he had been human, the dog would have uttered a deep sigh. There was no accounting for the man's whims. But Charlie did return, staring up with hungry eyes.

"They'll be comin' for you. How long, you reckon? Day or two?"

The old hand shook as it settled on Charlie's head.

"Ain't no reason to put on like I don't care. Ain't no harm done if just for this little while . . ."

The old man's voice trailed off. Charlie nudged him.

"Hungry? That what you're telling me? Well, it's a feast you'll be havin' tonight."

With a flourish, the old man set a plate of meat on the floor. When it was gone, Charlie licked the hand that had fed him. His tail wagged. If the old man could be friendly, so could he. And friendly they were. The old man patted him, roughed his ears, and got down on his knees to wrestle with the dog. Charlie wagged, wriggled, licked, and barked to his heart's content. Not a gruff word was spoken.

"It's dark out. I ain't hankering to fight my way back without I can see good," Caleb said at last.

They spent the night where they were. After the man had seen to both mules, he made a pad of cured hides on the floor near the bed. Charlie curled up on the pad. Every once in a while, the dog would rouse to feel the old man's hand on his head. He would hear the old voice mutter, "Ain't no harm done if I *do* show I like the critter a mite. He'll be gone soon, anyway."

Charlie would doze again. There was no telling what people talked about, and no use losing sleep over it.

# 18

The inviting smell of bacon sizzling in a pan wakened Charlie. He stretched his legs, getting to his feet with some difficulty. The stiffness was worse, and his shoulder was sore again.

"Finally decided to move your lazy bones," Caleb grunted. But, in spite of the gruffness of his voice, he came over and scratched the back of Charlie's neck. Then he lifted the skillet from the stove, an old wood range, put some food down for Charlie, and some at the table for himself.

After breakfast, Caleb carefully spread the coals in the firebox. He closed the air vents and the damper in the stovepipe. These precautions to avoid any possibility of an unattended fire were instinctive after living in the wilderness so long.

"Gotta be sure nothing can still burn," he said. His voice had lost its gruffness, and Charlie liked the sound of it. He liked the way Caleb's face turned to look at him.

When they went out back, Caleb tied his shotgun to Betsy's back, cushioning it with a hide from the cabin. He studied the other mule for several minutes.

"Can't rightly leave you here to starve," he said. "I reckon you better come along, at least till I can talk to the sheriff about you."

Then the old man turned to Charlie. "Dog," he said, "you been around a long time without a name. I feel more comfort knowing you as Charlie. Maybe this critter needs a name, too."

Charlie listened, his head cocked to one side, a smile curling his mouth upward. How good it was to hear the warmth in Caleb's voice. How good to hear no anger. He gave a little sound of pleasure.

The old man sang as he tied the other mule behind Betsy.

"Oh, do you remember sweet Betsy from Pike? She crossed the high mountain with her lover, Ike . . ."

The song conveyed a sense of serenity as the four of them ambled up the trail, heading toward home. Occasionally Caleb's hand would drop onto Charlie's head. Charlie was so happy he frolicked like a puppy, holding the stiff leg up with its paw folded back. Now and then he stumbled over a branch or rock in the path.

"Don't get prancing too fancy!" Caleb grunted. The habit of grouching crept back, but his face shone with contentment.

When they arrived home, Betsy was led to her corner of the shed. The new animal was fractious and had to be tied in the corner Charlie had occupied. The dog looked from one mule to the other. He whined softly. Old Caleb didn't seem to notice Charlie's concern. He began again with his tuneless singing as he put grain in Betsy's bucket.

"Have to git another bucket for what's his name," he said.

He unearthed an old wooden box from the rubbish at the end of the grain bin.

"This'll do for now."

After the mules were fed, Caleb stood studying the new animal, scratching its nose, trying to make friends. But the mule only snorted and brayed, tossing his head and rolling his eyes.

"Ike! That's what you'll be!"

The old man's laughter rang out.

"Got me a Betsy, and here's me an Ike." His eyes saddened. "If only I could keep the big yaller dog!" He straightened his shoulders and glanced down. Charlie made a friendly little noise, thrusting his nose into the old man's hand.

"What you want?" Caleb groused, but he knelt

and took Charlie's ears in his two hands, tugging at them gently.

"Don't appear to be no more room out here," he continued. "Reckon you'll have to sleep inside."

He roughhoused with Charlie a little more, then patted the dog on the back.

"Come along, then," he said.

Charlie was wild with excitement when Caleb coaxed him into the cabin and made a pad of skins next to the bed.

In the days that followed, Charlie was fed from the table. Whatever the old man cooked for himself, he shared with the dog. He reached down bits of meat, and patted Charlie often. It made up for the dog's long period of loneliness. Caleb's hand reached down at night, too, as if to reassure the old man Charlie had not run away.

"No harm done," Caleb would mutter. "I 'spect, though, any day now . . ."

Each day they walked through the forest together. Now and then they would stop to check a trap.

"You want to be careful," the old man explained, holding up a trap to show Charlie how fast it closed.

"You don't eat none of the critter till I get it skinned. The furs'll pay for what else we need that we can't catch."

Then Caleb sighed and stared at the ground while Charlie yipped, impatient to go on. His leg grew stronger every day. He could almost run on all fours again.

Sometimes they would walk to a spot near the water. The old man would sit holding a fishing pole, dangling the line in the water. Charlie would doze beside him, waking to attention when the man stood to pull in a fish. He'd nose the fish before Caleb would put it into a bucket of water.

At dusk one evening, there was a knock at the door. The old man was stirring a stew on the stove.

"Sssssst!" he whispered to the dog.

The pounding at the door grew louder. At last the old man went to open it a crack. He peered out, then opened the door wider. He appeared relieved.

"Come by yourself?" he asked heartily. "Come in and set a spell."

"Don't I always come alone?" the sheriff asked. "you expecting someone else?"

Caleb swallowed hard, but said nothing. He put bowls of food on the table, and a generous helping on the floor for Charlie. While he worked, the sheriff questioned him about the other poacher.

"He weren't a bad sort. Saved the dog, or at least give me enough time so's I could rescue him. Wouldn't let his friend Buck get off another shot at Charlie."

"Nonetheless, he shot deer out of season. According to Buck, he set up the whole operation, including buyers down in Lynxtown."

"Buck! Hmph!"

"I didn't think you'd believe his story. But I have to check it out."

The old man could offer no help in that regard. He'd seen the man only once, and argued that he had probably put a lot of distance between himself and his former partner.

"That Buck's a mean and vengeful one!"

It wasn't until the sheriff got up to leave that the old man ventured to ask, "I 'spect you ain't heard nothing from those two as lost the dog?"

The sheriff cleared his throat.

"I've been pretty busy since I took Buck in. I didn't get a letter off to them until yesterday."

Caleb looked at the sheriff and blinked. Then he looked at the floor.

"I'm sorry, Caleb. I had to notify them. It's part of my job."

After the sheriff left, the old man lit the kerosene lamp and sat at the table with a book. Betsy brayed. So did Ike. He interrupted his reading to go out and feed the mules. Charlie lay, full and content, looking out the open door.

When the old man came back inside, he shoved the book across the table.

"C'mere, pooch," he said.

# 19

It had been a good day. Caleb and Charlie had spent the entire afternoon by the stream. The old man whistled as they walked back to the cabin. The bucket he carried was heavy with fish. Charlie was beginning to like the smell of them. Hearing something, the man stopped whistling. Voices were audible above the late afternoon sounds of the forest.

"Bound to happen. Might's well be soon as late," the old man commented. The gruffness returned to his voice.

Charlie nosed Caleb's hand and was surprised when it drew away. They walked in silence, Charlie subdued by Caleb's distant manner. When they were almost in the clearing, the dog recognized the scent of the friendly sheriff on the wind. And, mingling with it were other scents, strange, yet somehow familiar.

The dog bounded eagerly as he recognized, first by smell, then by sound, and a few seconds later by sight, the people he had not seen for more than nine months.

Maggie ran to meet him, crying, "Charlie! Charlie! Oh, Charlie!"

Limping and leaping, the dog ran to her. He jumped up, resting his good paw on her shoulder, licking her face while his tail wagged in furious circles. She put her arms around him, tears trickling down her face.

"Charlie! Charlie!" she repeated.

Claire Dawson fumbled in her purse for a tissue to dry her eyes. She ran to hug Charlie, too.

"We were so afraid you might have died," she said.

Caleb stomped to the door of the cabin. Sheriff Alderman stopped him.

"Maggie, Claire, meet Caleb. He's the one who saved your dog when the poacher almost killed him."

"Evenin'," Caleb said.

He gave a curt nod, then strode past and into the cabin. The door slammed with resounding force. Charlie followed, limping slightly. He scratched at the door.

"Git!" came the cross voice from inside.

Charlie pawed harder, demanding to be let in. The old man could be heard banging a pot on the stove. Maggie went to the step, stooping to put her arms around Charlie. He turned and nuzzled her neck, making happy noises. She drew back and let her fingers examine the scar on his shoulder, now almost hidden in his thick fur.

"Look, Mom," she said. "This is why he's limping."

Her mother bent to look at it, and shuddered.

If it hadn't been for the old man . . . She didn't finish the thought. "Maggie, we owe Caleb a great deal for what he's done."

Turning to the sheriff, she said, "I want to pay him for his trouble."

A frown knotted the sheriff's brow, and he shook his head.

"Caleb wouldn't count it trouble to care for a needy animal."

Claire Dawson opened her purse and pulled out the dog collar.

"Thank you for saving this for us, Sheriff. Thank you for everything you've done."

She slipped the collar around Charlie's neck. He tossed his head and fought against it, as if he didn't like the feel of it.

"I'd like to leave some money with you, Sheriff. For the old man, I mean," Claire Dawson persisted.

The sheriff stared at her for a moment.

"It's hard enough for Caleb as it is. Don't make it any worse," he said firmly.

She looked distressed.

"I guess he has grown fond of our Charlie."

"You might say that," the sheriff responded curtly. Then he commented, "We'd better get you back down to your car. It can get dark in a hurry around here."

"I suppose you're right."

She looked down at Charlie, who had gone back to scratching at the door and whining to be let in. She looked at Maggie's troubled expression and slipped her arm around her daughter.

"We have to go," she said softly.

"But Mom, I haven't even had a chance to thank Caleb."

The sheriff smiled. "You'll be here a long time if you plan to wait for Caleb to come out of his cabin."

"Well," Maggie's mother said tentatively. Then her face set with resolution. "We really can't stay here all night."

Maggie stood quietly petting Charlie and ruffling his fur.

"It won't help matters to wait until it's too dark for us to see our way out."

Mrs. Dawson started walking across the clearing. "Come on, Maggie. Come, Charlie."

Maggie lifted her hand to knock at the door, but when she heard another banging sound, dropped it to Charlie's collar. She followed her mother, tugging Charlie with her. The sheriff turned to go, calling back, "I'll be by in a day or two."

"Don't put yourself out none," Caleb shouted bitterly.

Hearing the old man, Charlie yipped, yanked free, and hurried back to the cabin.

Claire Dawson turned and patted her leg.

"Charlie! Come!" she said. She looked determined. "His discipline has been totally forgotten."

Charlie answered her with a bark. He ran to them, then back to the steps. He sat there and yipped.

"Maggie, we'll have to take a very firm hand with him!"

The sheriff's eyes began to smile. He gave Claire Dawson a direct look.

"Like you did when he got lost here in the first place?"

Claire Dawson lifted her chin and returned his steady gaze.

"We waited for him as long as we could. We nearly got caught in the snow as it was. It was a terrible blizzard."

The sheriff said nothing further. Shadows were blending into a patterned darkness.

"Charlie!" Maggie cried, running to him. "Please come with us."

Charlie jumped up and licked her face. But his head turned back to the cabin. Nothing was heard from inside, and no light shone out the window. Charlie went a little way with Maggie, then turned and ran back to the step in front of the cabin. He began whining and running back and forth from Maggie to the cabin door.

"Sheriff?" Claire Dawson appealed.

The sheriff shrugged. "As far as I can see, the dog's not breaking any laws. I can hardly arrest him. And Caleb's in the clear."

"I just meant . . ." Mrs. Dawson began.

Then, setting her jaw with determination, she strode back across the clearing. She rapped sharply at the door. There was no answer. Charlie scratched and barked again, then turned and yipped up at Claire. Claire Dawson knocked harder, looking desperately toward the dark window.

Maggie, sensing Charlie's distress, turned Charlie's face up to hers and spoke soothingly. "I know he loves you, Charlie. It's just, he can't say good-bye to you." She rubbed her hands up over his ears, then tried to push the corners of his mouth up into a smile.

"You'll have fun at home. I promise you. I got something really special for you to have when you get there."

Charlie pulled away and scratched at the door again.

"It's just, he's sad you're leaving, Charlie,"

Maggie explained patiently. "I know how he feels. I thought I'd die of lonesomeness when you got lost."

Claire Dawson beat loudly at the door with both her fists.

"Mr. — er, Caleb. Please."

The door opened a crack and Caleb thrust his face out. He glared, but said nothing.

"He — our dog — Charlie won't leave," she said.

"Ain't my concern."

"But if you told him to go?" Mrs. Dawson asked.

Maggie looked up at the old man, her eyes pleading.

"Could you, maybe, please?"

The door opened a trifle more.

"What you want I should do?" Caleb asked in a controlled voice, trying to ignore Charlie's insistent nose in his hand.

"Could you just explain to him," Maggie asked. "He'll go if you tell him to."

Caleb cleared his throat. His hand touched Maggie's head for a minute, then drew back. He looked at Charlie and let out his breath with a heavy sigh. Then his face twisted as if in anger, and he pointed at the dog.

"Git!" he said.

Charlie just whined and nuzzled the old man's hand.

"Git!" Caleb said again, but the dog did not budge.

The old man reached down and picked up a stick. He raised it over his head. Charlie barked and wagged his tail.

"Git!"

Then the stick came down. The dog barked again, and his tail stopped wagging. But the stick stopped inches from Charlie's nose. Caleb groaned and threw the stick as far away as he could. He dropped to his knees and put his arms around Charlie. He buried his face in the dog's fur.

"You knowed I couldn't hit you."

The old shoulders shook, and his face remained hidden against Charlie's shoulder.

"I was always fussed about hittin' you that one time. Even when you ate that 'coon out of my trap, I was still sorry, and wanted to make friends with you, such a lonely critter you was."

The old man paused and breathed deeply. He lifted his head and looked at Charlie. "It was just, I always knew this day'd be comin'. I knew your folks'd come to claim you, and I couldn't bear the thought of it."

He cleared his throat and swiped at his eyes with the back of his hand.

"But hit you again? Never!"

Claire Dawson looked silently at her shoes, looked away at the bird feeder in the cedar tree at the edge of the clearing, looked toward the sheriff. She made no attempt to hide her tears.

Tears streamed down Maggie's face, too, and she struggled to control her voice when she spoke.

"Charlie doesn't want to leave Caleb, Mom," she said. "And it's only fair. Caleb saved his life."

She put her arms around both the dog and the man. Her hands trembled as she took off the collar and kissed Charlie on the nose.

"I guess he's your dog now, not ours," she said. "I'll . . . I'll get another puppy. I guess I can learn to love it just as much."

She patted her mother's shoulder. "It'll be OK, Mom," she reassured her. They started to cross the clearing together.

Maggie turned to wave back at the man and the dog.

"I'll come back to see you, Charlie. And Caleb, I'll write to you about the new puppy. Maybe I can even bring it to show you both."

Charlie whined, but then he turned to lick Caleb's hand. Together, they watched the three people disappear among the trees.

# About the Author

Born in Iowa, ANN DORO attended the University of Northern Iowa. Later she received a B.A. from California State University of Northridge and an M.A. from Loyola University in Westchester, California. She has published poetry in a number of quarterlies. Her stories for children have appeared in *Highlights for Children* and *Action*. She also has a TV credit. While a teacher, she enjoyed teaching creative writing to her third- and fourth-grade students. She also teaches adults in an ongoing writing workshop.

# APPLE®PAPERBACKS

# *Pick an Apple and Polish Off Some Great Reading!*

**NEW APPLE TITLES**

| | | | |
|---|---|---|---|
| ☐ | MT41917-X | Darci in Cabin 13 Martha Tolles | $2.75 |
| ☐ | MT42193-X | Leah's Song Eth Clifford | $2.50 |
| ☐ | MT40409-1 | Sixth Grade Secrets Louis Sachar | $2.75 |
| ☐ | MT41732-0 | Too Many Murphys Colleen O'Shaughnessy McKenna | $2.75 |

**BESTSELLING APPLE TITLES**

| | | | |
|---|---|---|---|
| ☐ | MT42709-1 | Christina's Ghost Betty Ren Wright | $2.75 |
| ☐ | MT41042-3 | The Dollhouse Murders Betty Ren Wright | $2.50 |
| ☐ | MT42319-3 | The Friendship Pact Susan Beth Pfeffer | $2.75 |
| ☐ | MT40755-4 | Ghosts Beneath Our Feet Betty Ren Wright | $2.50 |
| ☐ | MT40605-1 | Help! I'm a Prisoner in the Library Eth Clifford | $2.50 |
| ☐ | MT41794-0 | Katie and Those Boys Martha Tolles | $2.50 |
| ☐ | MT40283-8 | Me and Katie (The Pest) Ann M. Martin | $2.50 |
| ☐ | MT40565-9 | Secret Agents Four Donald J. Sobol | $2.50 |
| ☐ | MT42883-7 | Sixth Grade Can Really Kill You Barthe DeClements | $2.75 |
| ☐ | MT42882-9 | Sixth Grade Sleepover Eve Bunting | $2.75 |
| ☐ | MT41118-7 | Tough-Luck Karen Johanna Hurwitz | $2.50 |
| ☐ | MT42326-6 | Veronica the Show-off Nancy K. Robinson | $2.75 |
| ☐ | MT42374-6 | Who's Reading Darci's Diary? Martha Tolles | $2.75 |

Available wherever you buy books...
or use the coupon below.

Scholastic Inc., P.O. Box 7502, 2932 East McCarty Street, Jefferson City, MO 65102

Please send me the books I have checked above. I am enclosing $_____ (please add $2.00 to cover shipping and handling). Send check or money order — no cash or C.O.D.'s please.

Name_____

Address_____

City _____ State/Zip _____

Please allow four to six week for delivery. Offer good in the U.S.A. only.
Sorry, mail order not available to residents of Canada. Prices subject to change.

APP589